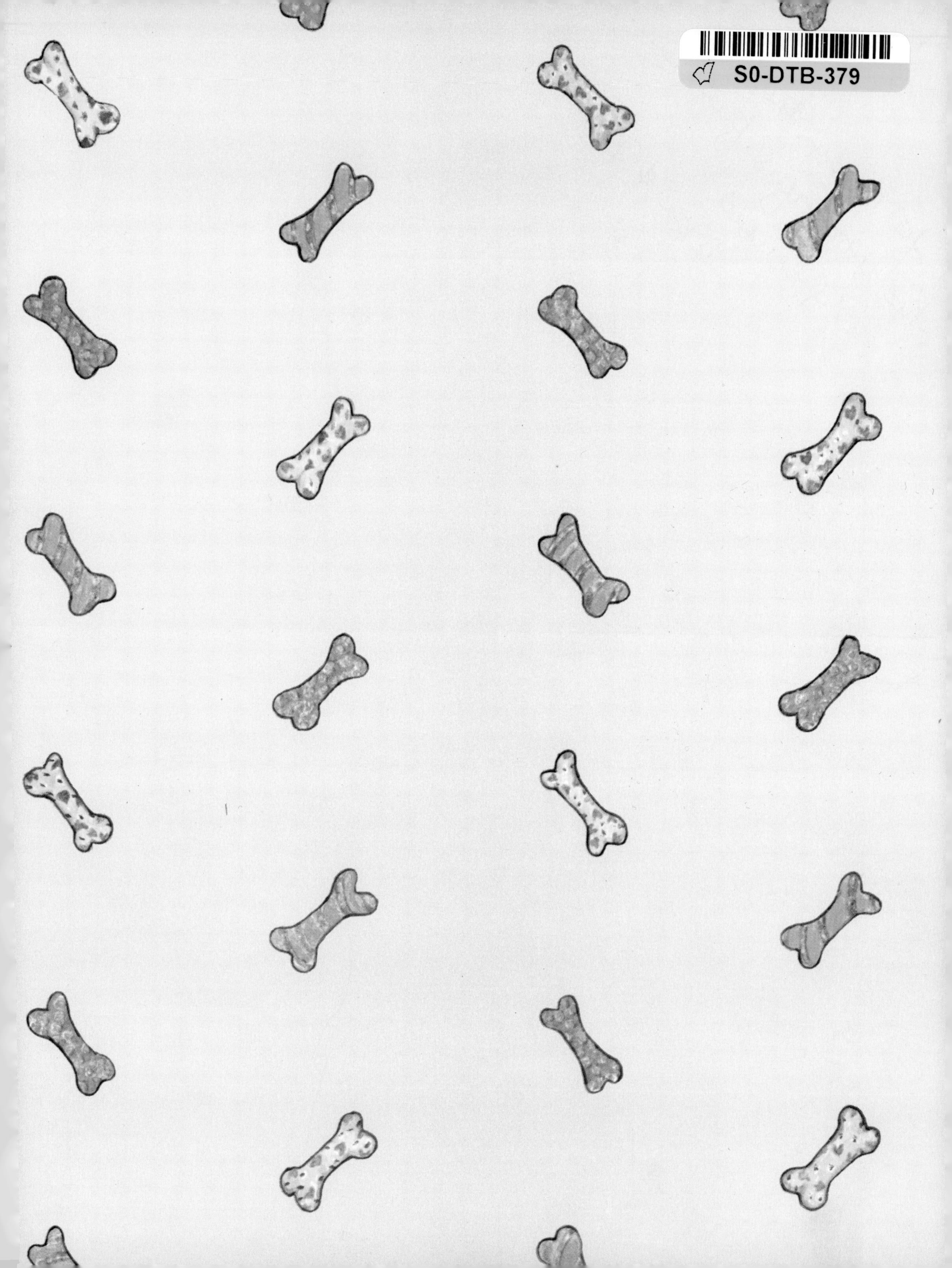
S0-DTB-379

for Brady and
his wonderful friend...
love you,
Mom & Dad

Library of Congress Cataloging-in-Publication Data: West, Cathy. The best place in the world. SUMMARY: After traveling with his parents to a snowy mountain, a forest campground, and a huge amusement park, Little Wrinkle decides that the best place in the world is with the ones you love. [1. Travel—Fiction] I. Scribner, Toni, Ill. II. Title. PZ7. W5174Be 1986 [E] 86-6555 ISBN: 0-394-88431-0 Manufactured in the United States of America 1 2 3 4 5 6 7 8 9 0

Sparkler Books is an imprint of Pharos Books, a Scripps Howard Company.

The Best Place in the World

A Wrinkles Storybook

by Cathy West
illustrated by Toni Scribner

Random House/Sparkler Books

Copyright © 1986 Ganz Bros. Toys.

Licensed by United Feature Syndicate, Inc.

All rights reserved under International and Pan-American Copyright Conventions. Published in the United States by Random House, Inc., New York, and simultaneously in Canada by Random House of Canada Limited, Toronto.

Little Wrinkle sprawled in front of the fireplace one rainy afternoon with the newspaper scattered all around him. He couldn't read much yet, but that didn't matter. He still liked to look at the newspaper. For one thing, his father was the editor of the paper. And every page was filled with pictures of famous people and faraway places. When Little Wrinkle looked at the pictures, he pretended he was someone different and someplace different—not just Little Wrinkle, stuck in the same old house in the same old town with nothing new to do.

Little Wrinkle looked up at his father. "Papa," he said, "where's the best place in the world?"

"Hmmm," said Papa. "There are a lot of nice places in the world. It would be hard to choose just one."

Little Wrinkle climbed onto his father's lap. "Come on, Papa, try hard. You've been to lots of places. What's your favorite?"

Mama laid her book aside. "I don't know about you," she said, "but I've always wanted to go to the mountains. I love snow."

"Me, too," said Little Wrinkle. "Papa, could we ever go to the mountains? Could we?"

"Well," said Papa, "as a matter of fact, your mother and I have been thinking about taking a trip."

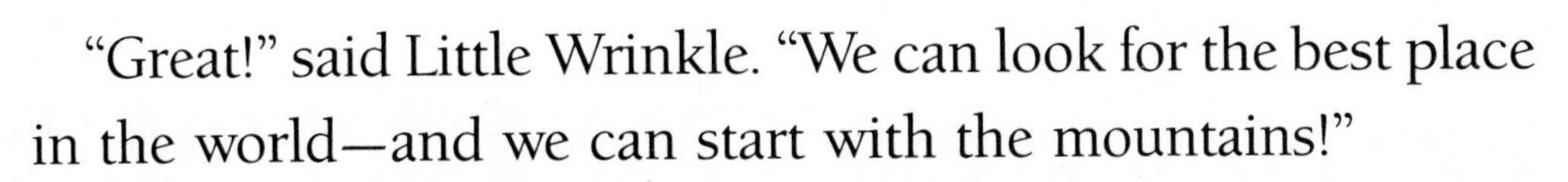

"Great!" said Little Wrinkle. "We can look for the best place in the world—and we can start with the mountains!"

Papa laughed, but then he said, "You know, that's a good idea. It would make a wonderful front-page story for my newspaper ...'The Wrinkles Family Finds the Best Place in the World.'"

So the very next morning they hopped on a plane and flew to Flurry Mountain.

"This is great!" said Little Wrinkle as he looked around. Huge snowflakes floated gently from the sky like white butterflies. All around them people in brightly colored hats and scarfs and snowsuits were playing in the snow.

First the Wrinkles went sledding.

Then they went skiing.

Then they went ice skating. "You won't fall, Little Wrinkle—we'll help you," said his parents. "Here, hold on to our hands."

But Little Wrinkle's favorite thing of all was the snowman-building contest.

"Now, the thing to do," said Mama, "is to put our heads together, come up with an original idea, plan the design..."

But Little Wrinkle had already started! He took tiny snowballs and rolled them around and around until they became big snowballs. So big that Papa had to help push them.

"Whew!" said Papa. "Don't you think three's enough?"

"No! More! More!" shouted Little Wrinkle. By the time he stopped, eight huge snowballs stood in a crooked row.

"What in the world are we going to do with all these!" said Papa.

"It looks like a giant snake!" said Mama.

"You are almost right," Little Wrinkle told his mother. And then he whispered his plan to his parents. "Do you think we can do it?"

"Yes, it's a wonderful idea," said Mama.

"Let's get started!" said Papa.

First they lined up seven of the big snowballs into a curvy S shape. They heaved the eighth snowball on top of the first.

Then each of them took charge of a different task. Little Wrinkle gathered some pine branches that had fallen to the ground. Mama donated her bright red scarf with the fringe on the ends. Papa collected an armful of icicles that hung from the lodge roof like teeth.

"Hurry!" cried Little Wrinkle. "There's not much time left!"

"Thweet!" The judge blew her whistle. "Time's up!" Carefully she studied every entry. The Wrinkles family held hands—and their breath—as they waited for the judge's choice.

"The first-place winner is—the Wrinkles family!" shouted the judge. "For their fantastic...ferocious...fire-breathing... snow dragon!"

The crowd clapped and cheered. "Hurray!" shouted Little Wrinkle. Together they had won the blue ribbon!

But by then their gloves were a bit wet and their toes were tingling from the cold, so they hurried into the lodge. In front of a roaring fire, they celebrated their victory with steaming mugs of hot chocolate.

"I think this is the best place in the world!" said Little Wrinkle.

"We certainly have had fun," said Mama.

But the next morning Papa woke up with the sniffles. And he didn't much feel like going out into the cold.

"This place is very nice," he said. "But it's not *quite* my idea of the best place in the world."

"Where would *you* like to go, Papa?" asked Little Wrinkle.

"Someplace nice and warm!" said Papa. "I know just the spot."

The Wrinkles left Flurry Mountain that very day. Their next stop was Sunshine Campgrounds.

When they arrived, they set up their tent. Little Wrinkle helped.

Later they got out their fishing poles. The warm, bright sun made the stream glisten like diamonds.

"Just smell those pine trees!" said Papa. "This is the life."

The Wrinkles spent the whole afternoon fishing. Little Wrinkle caught a big catfish. Mama caught a little catfish. Papa caught an old boot.

"Well," said Papa, "not everybody can catch a boot with a worm!" Mama and Little Wrinkle laughed.

Later they hiked up into the hills and Mama taught Little Wrinkle the names of some of the trees. When they reached the top, they stopped for a picnic lunch. They were so high up they could see for miles, and the roads and fields below looked like a giant's patchwork quilt.

That evening they built a crackling campfire that sent sparks shooting up into the dark sky. Papa showed Little Wrinkle how to toast marshmallows on the end of a long green stick. Mama told a ghost story and Little Wrinkle taught his parents a song he'd learned in school. Then Papa put out the fire and everyone snuggled up in the tent. The woods were so quiet, it was easy to go to sleep.

But just after midnight Little Wrinkle woke up. He heard a sound outside. A spooky-rustly-scratchy sound! He jumped on Papa's sleeping bag and began to pull his father's ears. "Papa! Wake up! Something's trying to get us!"

"Don't worry," said Papa, rubbing his eyes. "I'll go look. Hand me my knapsack." And he went out into the darkness.

Suddenly there was a noise and something flashed! Mama and Little Wrinkle peeked out through the tent flaps..

"I got him!" they heard Papa shout through the darkness. "What a great shot!"

"You...shot him?" said Little Wrinkle.

"Yes," said Papa. "I shot his picture!"

"Whose picture?" said Mama.

"The raccoon's picture," said Papa. "He was looking for food. Raccoons do most of their hunting at night, you know."

"Wow!" said Little Wrinkle. "Can I take the picture to school to show all my friends?"

"Sure," said Papa. He tucked Little Wrinkle back into his sleeping bag and kissed him good night.

"We sure had a lot of fun together today," said Little Wrinkle as he drifted off to sleep. "I think maybe this...is the best place in the...world...."

But after several days in the woods, Little Wrinkle began to grow tired of eating catfish. "This place has been wonderful," he said. "But I'm still not sure it's *exactly* the best place. Can we go someplace else and may I pick it?"

"Of course you may!" said Papa. "Where would you like to go?"

"I know just the place!" Little Wrinkle shouted, and he began to drag their camping gear to the car.

In a few hours they turned into a parking lot filled with thousands of cars. They were at Funland—the greatest amusement park in the world! Balloons filled the sky. Silly clowns welcomed them through the gate.

"This place is the best!" cried Little Wrinkle. It had the funniest funhouse...

twenty-eight flavors of cotton candy...

and the wildest roller coaster they had ever seen!

Little Wrinkle was leading his parents over to the merry-go-round when he heard a voice boom over the loudspeaker: "The Funland Parade is about to begin. Everybody join in!"

"Come on!" shouted Little Wrinkle. He was so excited, he raced ahead of his parents.

"Little Wrinkle!" his mother called. "Don't go too far ahead of us!"

"I won't," he said without even looking back.

"This is definitely the best place in the world!" Little Wrinkle thought to himself as the parade snaked in and out among the rides.

THE FUNLAND PARADE

Finally the parade ended. Some of the people hurried to catch one last ride. Others gathered to go home. Little Wrinkle turned to tell his mother that he never wanted to leave—but the woman beside him wasn't his mother!

Little Wrinkle whirled around, but he couldn't see his parents anywhere! His lip began to quiver and he felt like crying. What should he do?

He ran to the merry-go-round. His parents weren't there.

"Maybe they're waiting for me by the cotton candy stand," he thought. But they weren't there, either.

He hurried past the funhouse. It looked scarier now that he was all alone.

Little Wrinkle was starting to get all mixed up. Hadn't he already come this way before? He couldn't remember. Everything was beginning to look the same to him.

Then he saw a Funland security guard giving some people directions. Little Wrinkle had asked his mother about the man's uniform when they first arrived.

Little Wrinkle ran over to the guard. "Can you help me?" he asked the man. "My name is Little Wrinkle...and I've lost my parents!"

"Don't you worry," said the guard. "We'll find them right away." Together they walked to the entrance gate. A woman with a Funland badge called over the loudspeaker: "Mama and Papa Wrinkle—please come to the front gate!"

Little Wrinkle waited nervously. Had his parents heard the message? Would they come and get him?

"Little Wrinkle! Sweetheart! There you are!" It was Mama and Papa. Little Wrinkle flew into their arms. Their hugs felt better than anything.

"You know what?" he said to his parents.

"What?" asked Mama and Papa.

"*I* know where the best place in the world is."

"Where?" asked his parents.

"Anywhere," said Little Wrinkle, "as long as I'm with you."

Back home the next day, Little Wrinkle said to his father, "I'm sorry you didn't get a big story for your newspaper."

"But I did," said Papa. "And you can help me write it."

Papa sat down in front of his typewriter. He pulled Little Wrinkle onto his lap. Mama looked over their shoulders as Little Wrinkle helped his father type out the headline:

THE BEST PLACE IN THE WORLD
IS WITH THE PEOPLE YOU LOVE!

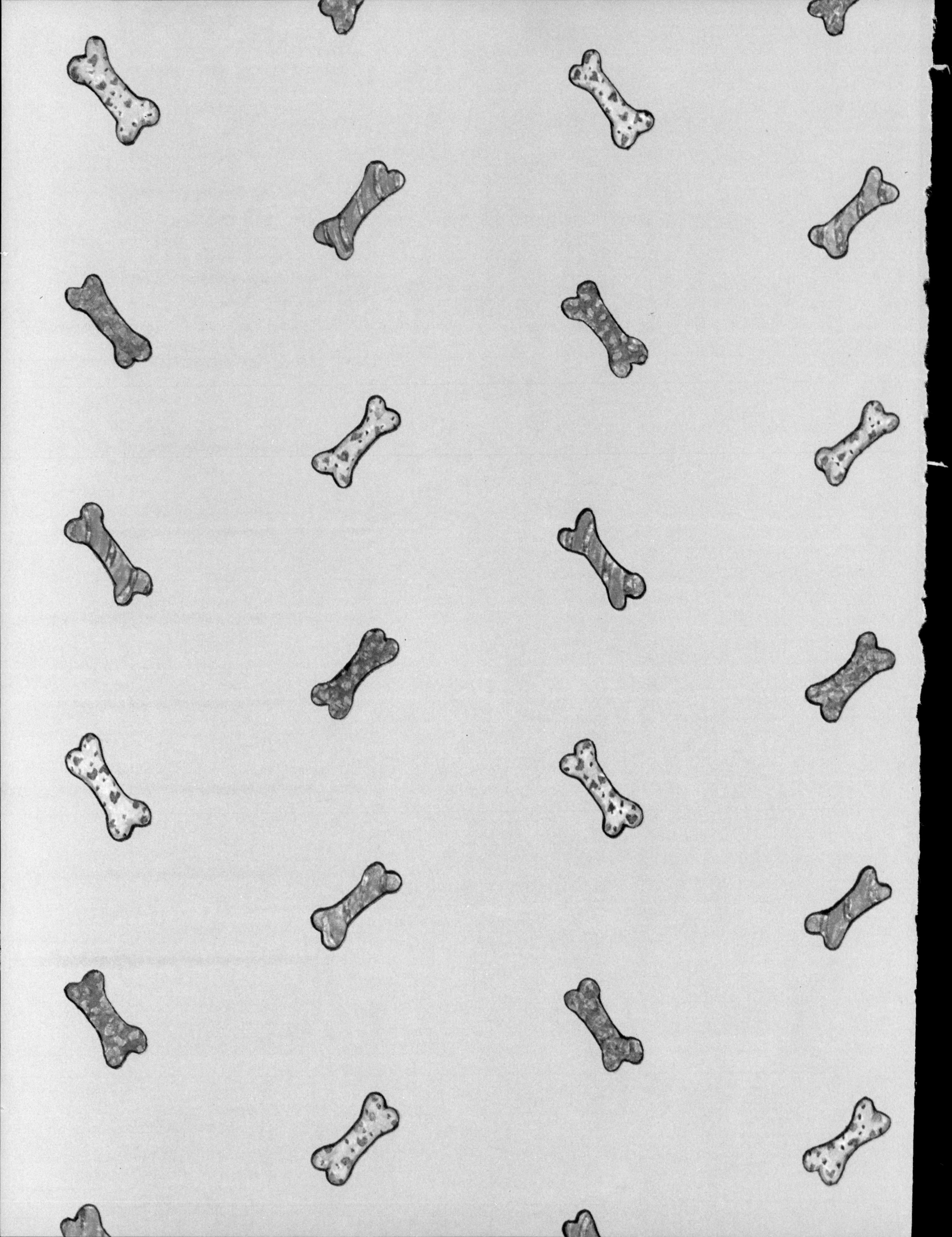